For my father, John Harrison — D. L. H.

To Andree — N. D.

Library of Congress Cataloging in Publication Data. Harrison, David Lee. Detective Bob and the great ape escape.
SUMMARY: A frolicsome ape eludes Detective Bob's efforts to return him to his cage in the zoo.
[1. Apes—Fiction. 2. Zoological gardens—Fiction. 3. Stories in rhyme] I. Delaney, Ned. II. Title.
PZ8.3.H2432De   [E] 80–10584   ISBN 0–8193–1031–X   ISBN 0–8193–1032–8 lib. bdg.

DETECTIVE BOB
AND
THE GREAT
APE ESCAPE

by DAVID L. HARRISON

pictures by NED DELANEY

Parents Magazine Press
New York

Hey! I think
that clever ape
may be trying
to escape!

Call the keeper
of the zoo!
He will know
just what to do!

You say I have
a missing ape?
How ever could
that ape escape?
This is not
my lucky day.
I cannot let him
get away!

Do not worry.
Do not fear.
The great
Detective Bob
is here!

That ape is gone
without a trace.
I'm glad to have you
on this case!

We're from TV—
Channel 3.
Where do you think
that ape could be?

We're the Press,
Detective Bob.
We'd like your picture
on this job.

Hurry, please.
I've work to do
to find the ape
and save the zoo.

That ape is smart.
That ape is quick.
That ape will try
to play a trick.

I will find him.
You will see.
Come along
and follow me.
We will look
in every place
until we find
that missing face.

Do you think
an ape would creep
inside a pen
that's full of sheep?

He isn't there.
It's plain to me
that pen is not
where he would be.

Would he try
to hide in there
and make us think
that he's a bear?

BEAR

If he tried it,
I would know.
He isn't there—
and so we'll go.

That giraffe
is not too tall.
I don't think
he belongs at all.

An ape in there?
Don't make me laugh!
Read the sign.
It says GIRAFFE!

Does a hippo
look like that?
I thought a hippo
had more fat.

An ape would never
risk a fuss
with any
hippopotamus.

That's a
funny-looking seal.
Do you think
that seal's for real?

We detectives
know a lot.
That's a seal.
An ape it's not.

A lion is
supposed to roar.
He's never beat
his chest before.

An ape would never
go inside
a lion's den
and try to hide.

Do you think
he'd stop awhile
to hide beside
a crocodile?

A crocodile
would bite and snap
if anyone
disturbed his nap.

That ape is smart.
That ape is quick.

That ape is sly.
That ape is slick.

I know that ape
is here someplace.
Bob, you have to
crack this case!

Do not worry.
Do not fret.
Don't give up.
I'll find him yet.

See that camel?
See his hump?
See—he has
an extra lump!

That hump was there
when he was bought
at Honest Al's
Used Camel Lot.

Detective Bob,
come over here.
Here's a
funny-looking deer.

That is just
a deer, my dear.
An ape would not
escape in here.

Listen! Have you
ever heard
such a silly-
sounding bird?

An ape was never
built to fly.
An ape's too smart
to even try.

That's a
funny-looking moose.
Could that be
the ape that's loose?

You'd better stick
with Channel 3
and leave this
missing ape to me.

That elephant
is awfully small
to be an elephant
at all!

An ape could never
grow a trunk.
That elephant
has only shrunk.

Aha! I think
I've found a clue!
Call the keeper
of the zoo!

Bob, you've found
our ape at last!
Close his cage
and lock it—fast!

Aha! I've found
your missing ape!
Aha! Your ape
did not escape!

Our missing ape
is back to stay!
Detective Bob,
you saved the day!

I've done another
super job.
No one fools
Detective Bob!

ABOUT THE AUTHOR

DAVID L. HARRISON lives near Springfield, Missouri, just across the road from a number of cows. He says, "I have one of everything I need — a wife, a daughter, and a son — as well as quite a few things I don't need. My favorite things to do are writing stories, sitting on an island, and eating homemade ice cream. My biggest wish is to do all three at the same time."

Detective Bob and the Great Escape is the 133rd story he has written over the last twenty years. And it is one of his more than two dozen published books. Mr. Harrison confesses to liking Detective Bob, even though — or maybe especially because — Bob's so silly.

ABOUT THE ARTIST

NED DELANEY reports, "I knew when I began to draw the ape for this book it had to be somewhat real looking, that it couldn't be like the animals in my own books, which I disguise with clothes and human features. So I took my camera and sketchbook and went off to the two zoos in the Boston area, where I live. Neither one had an ape. I solved my ape problem when I found a postcard of a stuffed gorilla."

Mr. Delaney has been writing and illustrating picture books since graduating from college. For the past few years he has also been teaching children's book writing and illustration at local colleges.